FALL
A Tale of What's to Come

by *Janet McDonnell*
illustrated by Linda Hohag

created by Wing Park Publishers

 CHILDRENS PRESS ®
CHICAGO

Library of Congress Cataloging-in-Publication Data

McDonnell, Janet, 1962-
 Fall : a tale of what's to come / by Janet McDonnell ; illustrated by
Linda Hohag.
  p.   cm. — (The Four seasons)
 Summary: Mouse wonders why all of his woodland friends are too
busy to play until Ground Hog explains that they are preparing for
what's to come.
  ISBN 0-516-00676-2 (lib. bdg.)
  [1. Autumn—Fiction. 2. Animals—Fiction.] I. Hohag, Linda, ill.
II. Title. III. Series: McDonnell, Janet, 1962-   Four seasons.
 PZ7.M478436Fal   1993
 [E]—dc20
                                                  93-20171
                                                    CIP
                                                    AC

FALL
A Tale of What's to Come

One chilly morning, Mouse popped his
head out from his home under a tree stump.
"What a great day," he said. "Hey, Squirrel,
let's play tag!"

"Play?" said Squirrel. "Who has time to play? I have things to do! Nuts to gather!" And off he went.

"What a grouch!" thought Mouse. "I didn't want to play with him anyway."

Just then, Mouse saw Chipmunk. He was gathering nuts too, and stuffing them in his cheeks. Mouse giggled. "Chipmunk, you look silly," he said.

"Why there's nothing silly about it," said Chipmunk. "I'm getting ready for what's to come. And you'd better get ready too, or you'll be sorry."

"What do you mean?" asked Mouse. "What's coming up?" But Chipmunk did not hear him. He was off looking for more nuts. "Hmmm," thought Mouse. "All those nuts must be going to his head."

As Mouse wandered the forest, looking for friends, he heard a twittering racket overhead. Looking up, he saw that the trees were filled with bright little swallows, all chirping together.

"Hey, what's this, a party?" asked Mouse.

"No, no," said a swallow. "We are making plans for what's to come."

"We're taking a trip," said another. "We're all flying south. And we have to be going soon. The leaves are already red and orange."

The swallow was right. Mouse looked at
the bright, beautiful colors. He watched one,
then another, then another pretty leaf float
to the ground.

One floated right past his nose. "What's this?" he asked. "There's a caterpillar on this leaf! You poor little fellow. Would you like me to climb up and put your leaf back?"

"Oh, no," said Caterpillar. "I'm quite happy. I need to find a pile of leaves to crawl under to be ready for what's to come. So, if you please, put my leaf on the ground and I'll be on my way." Mouse did just that.

"Something funny is going on," he said to himself. "Something big is about to happen—but what?"

Mouse was thinking so hard that he almost bumped right into Ground Hog. "Well, hello!" said Mouse. "At last, someone to play tag with! Come on, Ground Hog, let's go!"

Then Mouse stopped and looked closely at his friend. "I don't mean to be rude," he said, "but you're getting pretty chubby. Maybe you should go on a diet."

Ground Hog chuckled. "You silly mouse," he said. "I'm getting fat on purpose. I'm getting ready for what's to come."

"What, what, WHAT'S to come?" said Mouse. "Please tell me! Why is everyone too busy to play? What is about to happen?"

"You mean you don't know?" said Ground Hog. "Autumn is here. Haven't you noticed?"

"Of course I have," said Mouse. "That is ... I mean ... what's autumn?"

"Autumn is Fall," said Ground Hog. "That's when the leaves fall from the trees. The air turns colder, and the night comes earlier."

"So. What's the big deal?" asked Mouse.

"When autumn comes, winter isn't far behind," said Ground Hog. "And there is a lot to do to get ready for winter. Soon snow will cover the ground and the plants will stop growing. Food will be hard to find. We have to either move to a different place or get ready for what's to come."

"Is that what Squirrel and Chipmunk were doing with all those nuts?" said Mouse.

"Yes," said Ground Hog. "They are storing away food for winter days."

"And I'll bet that's why the swallows are flying South," said Mouse.

"That's right," said Ground Hog. "The winter is warmer in the South. But Caterpillar will stay warm here under a blanket of leaves."

Suddenly Mouse began to worry. "Wait a minute," he said. "I'm not ready for winter! What should I do, Ground Hog? Tell me, what should I do?"

"Come with me," said Ground Hog. Mouse followed him to the edge of the forest. There was a great field of corn. A man on a machine was riding back and forth across the field.

"Look closely out there," said Ground Hog. "I think you'll get an idea."

Mouse squinted out at the field. He saw other mice running around behind the big machine.

Mouse looked confused. "You mean I should go play tag with the mice?"

"No, no, no," said Ground Hog. "They are not playing tag. They're gathering corn that the machine left behind. They will save it for later. That's what you should be doing. And you'll need to find a nice warm place to stay when the cold wind starts to blow."

"Oh, thank you," said Mouse. "Thank you for showing me what to do. I better get busy."

Just then, Mouse and Ground Hog heard
the crunch, crunch, crunch of human feet.
Quickly they hid behind a rock.

They saw four children walking by, all dressed in strange costumes. One was even dressed as a Mouse!

"What was that all about?" asked Mouse.

"I'm not sure," said Ground Hog. "But it happens every fall. The children dress in strange clothes and go door to door, filling up their bags with treats."

"Maybe they're getting ready for winter too," said Mouse.

"I don't think so," said Ground Hog. "They gobble up the treats right away. However, I do believe I'm about ready."

"What will you do?" asked Mouse.

"I'll crawl into my home underground and take a nice long nap until winter is over," said Ground Hog.

"For that long?" cried Mouse. "But I'm
going to miss you! And I'll miss the swallows,
and Caterpillar, and the leaves too! I don't
want winter to come. In fact, I'm not having

winter this year."

Ground Hog laughed. "I'm afraid you don't have a choice, Mouse. But you might just like winter."

29

Then Ground Hog yawned. "As for me, I'm looking forward to my little nap. Now, run along, Mouse. And don't be afraid."

Mouse gave Ground Hog a hug. "Good-by for now," he said.

"Good-by for now," said Ground Hog.

Then Mouse ran to join his friends in the field to prepare for what was to come. "Hey, wait for me!" he cried.

You have read what Mouse does in the fall.
Here's what children do.

Can you read these words?

play football

trick or treat

eat turkey and pumpkin pie

go back to school

jump in leaves

Can you think of other things?